What a delightful, entertaining, and romantic story! The narrative was clear from the beginning, and the outline of who the characters were gave extra clarity. I would heartily recommend 'The Perfect Stranger' *to anyone wanting a light read that flows well, is easy to read, and is enjoyable. Congratulations on such a delightful story, Judith.*

Di Riddell
Author 'Speak Out'

I loved the way you wove the story, like ships passing in the night, and finally to dock at the same destination.

Rita-Marie Lenton
Celebrant—SoulCrystalEarth; Author 'Creating A Fond Farewell'

The Perfect Stranger

Judith Waller

The Perfect Stranger
Copyright © 2023 Judith Waller
First published 2023

Disruptive Publishing
17 Spencer Avenue
Deception Bay QLD 4508
Australia
WEB: www.disruptivepublishing.com.au

Layout and editing by Jo Scott
Cover Illustration & Design, and incidental Illustrations by
David Wicks—DMW Creative Services
dave@dmwcreative.com.au
Photographs by Judith Waller

ISBN# 978-0-6457459-6-2 Print

The Perfect Stranger

A novella by

Judith Waller

Destiny:

A predetermined course of events

*– **your** destiny*

Dedicated to my long-time

husband, Mike Waller —

on whom the hero of the

story is loosely based.

ACKNOWLEDGEMENTS

A Vikings Tale
— poem by Karen and Ian Curtis (The Scurvy Dogs)

Thank you to my daughter, Trish Springsteen, for her invaluable assistance in the writing of this story.

Thank you to my husband, Mike Waller, for his assistance with the Pidgin English used throughout this story. (Any person living in Papua New Guinea (PNG) in the late 1960s to early 1970s learnt their Pidgin English from Police Superintendent Mike Thomas on a morning radio program, *Let's Talk Pidgin*.)

Many thanks to my editor, Jo Scott, who has done a mighty job and guided me all through, in a professional and friendly way.

Thanks also to my Beta readers, Di Riddell, Rita-Marie Lenton, and Lesley Oliver.

To the Illustrator – Many thanks to my very talented son, David Wicks, for the wonderful drawings and sketches— past and present—in particular for the cover of *The Perfect Stranger*

Thank you to Deborah Fay, Disruptive Publishing, for your assistance in the publication of my writings, much appreciated.

Table of Contents

CHARACTERS

Martin Lord
Electrical Mechanical Engineer and Sailor

Jennifer (Jenny) Lansing
Finance Specialist and Martin's love

Little Joe
Martin's boat boy

Ann Heywood
Jenny's trusted employee

Bob Cosgrove
Company Head and Jenny's boss

Jacquie Toms
Friend, and Papua New Guinea connection

Amanda
Ann's daughter

Jerry
Amanda's boyfriend

Ken
Ann's estranged husband

Geraldine
Jenny's receptionist

Connie
Jenny's secretary

Don Toms
Jacquie Toms' brother, and owner of Nuala Plantation

Nicky Toms
Don's wife, and co-owner of Nuala Plantation

Ian
Young man employed by Martin Lord

Jeff Hanson
Pilot

ONE

He was not a handsome man, but rather rugged and craggy looking as though he had withstood many a storm and rough seas. Tall in stature, with auburn hair, somewhat of the making of a Viking.

Martin stood on the stern of his sturdy yacht and looked back from whence he came. The desire in him was very strong, he loved the sea, but now he had another love and the image of her swept before his eyes once more with the memory of her snuggled in his arms.

He knew she loved him, but with the sea in his blood he could not, *would not*, ask her to join him. It was no life for a gentle woman used to the niceties of modern day living. So, the battle raged within him, he had left without uttering the words he knew she wanted to hear. With a sigh he turned and faced the sea ahead, he would try to write when he arrived back home.

Ah! Home ... how contradictory. Home for him was his yacht and the sea, not the little island with its lazy inhabitants that he had lived and worked around for some twenty-odd years. Yes! On the surface it appeared sleepy and quiet, but beneath the quiet exterior lay a lion waiting to spring and devour—the time would come when all hell would be let loose, another reason for keeping her away. To him she was too precious to be subjected to impending disaster.

'Masta! The wind she gets stronger, shall I set another reef in the main?' His little mate Joe's voice broke across his thoughts.

'Yes! Yes!' Martin replied. 'All looks good Little Joe—we will be in safe harbour by nightfall if this keeps up.'

Joe grinned at his master, then hurried off to do battle with the wind and the sails. He loved his job aboard the *Sinabada*. He had worked with Masta Lord for nearly ten years now, a native of the islands that Lord worked in and around; he knew them well and, like his Masta, loved the *Sinabada* and the sea she sailed upon. So named from the local language, meaning—

Sina (woman) and *bada* (good): Good woman

But! Now Joe was puzzled, there was truly something missing in his master's usually happy nature. Martin was quieter, and more serious, as if something weighed heavy on his mind. Joe hoped there was nothing greatly amiss. Of course, there was trouble brewing with the natives, and there had been for some time, but he and Martin were a strong team and had weathered many storms before, so surely this was no worse a threat. He shrugged his shoulders and turned his attention to the job at hand.

In the six days since they had left the northern shores of Australia and set course for the Bougainville Islands not much conversation had passed between them. Maybe things would be different when they reached home port.

Martin looked up at Little Joe just tying off the last reef. He thought to himself: a plucky little fellow, not the usual run-of-the mill native. Joe had a lot of sense to him, and Martin trusted him too. There wouldn't be many you could say that about.

Yep, sure hope the wind holds. In another hour they should see the home point, and another hour after that they should drop anchor in Jackson Bay. Then back to the grindstone of working life again.

It had been a good trip South. He had enjoyed seeing his family again, his two sisters and brothers. Life was being pretty kind to them all at the moment. Even his mother and father had looked well, for times had been hard for them in the past, and he knew he had contributed to some of that hardship.

Yes, this trip had been good for them all—but once again he struggled to keep *that* haunting image out of his mind.

* * * * *

TWO

Jennifer Lansing was tired. Her arms felt like lead as she negotiated the car down the sloping driveway. It was ten o'clock at night and she had just left the office, no wonder she felt worn out, like all the previous days it had been long and tiresome. Jenny enjoyed her work and the people around her, but she was very lonely.

Jenny steered expertly into the garage and killed the engine. She loved her home and the peace it offered her. It was a small place, very contemporary, built mainly of red cedar timber with a fully glassed front and rear, sitting high on the side of a hill overlooking a pine forest valley. Built on the outskirts of the city, it certainly gave her the peace and quiet that she craved after a hectic day.

Jenny managed a large branch office of a major finance corporation, called P.A.N. It had been a very rewarding job and she had worked hard to make it a success. Her handpicked staff, selected when she came to the position, were still with her and were extremely loyal, a credit to Jenny's own attitude to work. But now she felt unsettled and badly needed a rest. The two weeks' holiday north—taken under duress, with much pressure from her staff and other directors some six weeks earlier—had hardly been enough after the years of slogging without a break. Yes! Years it had been, having joined the company in the early 'fifties, she found it hard to realise the time had flown so fast.

It was now 1958, just a short eight years since she started with this company, no wonder she was tired; a break had been much needed. Jenny smiled to herself and allowed her thoughts to stray back to that holiday ...

* * *

She stopped the car in Cairns, as far north as she dared go, to allow a couple of days' vacation before the return trip. It was hot and she needed a place to cool off.

Flipping through the accommodation directory, she was startled by a gentle voice asking if she needed any help. Turning, she looked up into a pair of the nicest blue eyes, eyes full of concern that seemed to penetrate her very being. It seemed an eternity before she was able to collect herself and answer the voice and eyes. They belonged to a very tall, strong, rugged-looking man; tanned and weathered, a man of the sea, she assumed.

Then the oddest thing happened to her. Her upbringing went by the board. Her natural resistance to strangers disappeared and she felt safe with this stranger, suddenly able to communicate. She flashed him her nicest smile and her first words were, 'It's terribly hot and I am looking for a place to cool off.'

He immediately took charge—something that was also foreign to her. She was always the one in control and now someone else was taking over that role. It was a nice feeling. Two days of bliss! He had wined and dined, and ... yes, even bedded her. Oh! What a feeling that had been!

In that time Jenny had learned very little about him, only that he lived and worked in the islands in and around Papua New Guinea, or as the locals called it PNG. His name was Martin Lord. He had a yacht, and he loved the sea. Jenny would never forget him, and this was part of the reason for her unsettled feelings now ...

* * *

Quite suddenly a shrill noise cut across her thought waves. Jenny had been standing by her front door looking up at the stars. She fumbled with the door keys, then made a beeline for the phone.

'Hello,' she answered.

'Hi Jen, its Ann, did I get you out of bed?'

'Oh! Ann; no, I only just got in.'

'Jen, you will kill yourself. Ease up lady, you'll get no thanks for it.'

Ann Heywood was one of her most trusted employees, and a good friend besides, they had known each other for years. Ann had stood by Jenny through the final stages of her marriage breakup and ultimate divorce. She was always nagging her about how hard she worked.

The Managing Director of the company, Bob Cosgrove, was a bit of a sod and there was no love lost between he and Ann. Ann always thought he took advantage of the way Jenny worked, but Jenny and Bob had also been friends for years. They understood each other, so Jenny accepted Ann's comments as being concern for a friend.

'Okay Ann, what's the score? You did not ring at this time of night to tell me that I should not be working so hard.'

'Nothing really exciting Jen, can we have lunch tomorrow, just the two of us? There are a few things I need to talk over with you. Besides, I don't need a reason to ring a friend, do I?'

'Sorry Ann, I did not mean to snap. I guess I'm a little out of sorts these days.'

'You can shout that out! You still have not heard from him, have you?'

Ann knew all about Martin, Jenny had confided in her some weeks earlier.

'No Ann, I haven't, maybe I will never ever see or hear from him again.'

'Well girl, *do* something about it.'

'What! You mean go chasing halfway round the world after him? That's not my scene and you know it!'

'Jen look, it's not halfway round the world, it is only to the islands. Take a trip up there. It isn't a large place, you'll find him. You will only be holidaying, and he will never know you went there just for him. You know Jacquie Toms. Her brother has a plantation up that way; you could stay with them. Another break will do you the world of good, and who knows ... ?'

Jenny laughed, 'Ann, quit it, will you? I have too much on my plate to have another holiday right now, besides it costs you know! You don't do that sort of thing on peanuts. Let's drop it and I'll catch you for lunch tomorrow.'

'Okay Jen, see ya, bye.'

The other end of the line went dead, and Jenny hung up. Ann's suggestion was wild. Perhaps, she should try something like that! Jenny shook herself, crazy thing to think of anyway.

* * *

'You on the phone again Mum?' Ann's daughter Amanda had just raced into the sitting room as Ann was replacing the receiver. Amanda always raced everywhere—she never walked.

'Just talking with my boss, dear! You are home early tonight, aren't you?'

'Yes, I had a fight with Jerry, it's all off!'

Ann smiled to herself, Amanda and her boyfriend were always having a tiff, it was off, then it was on; a continual up-and-down relationship.

'No, dear! I have not seen him tonight,' this was in answer to her daughter's query regarding her father's whereabouts. Ann left the room, no longer smiling; she and Ken had been married for nearly twenty-five years and she knew it was over, there had been nothing between them for nearly five years. He had been getting more violent towards her and, to say the least, she was more than a little frightened of him. So why did they stay like this? She wished she was more like Jenny. In some ways she envied her.

Jenny had had the courage to make it on her own. Ann had watched while Jenny had struggled to hold her life together, finally leaving a toxic relationship with virtually nothing but the clothes she was wearing and the ability to work. And work she had! In the few years Jenny had been on her own she *had* made it: she had a lovely home and some investments, she commanded a high salary, and she was respected in the business world.

But! Ann could see beyond that; she could see the loneliness inside her friend. Oh! Yes, there were guys vying for Jenny's favours, but Jenny seemed totally unaware and ignored them all.

Ann felt that she lacked the courage to do what Jenny was doing so she put up with Ken and ignored his comings and goings. But now she was afraid the time was coming when there had to be a break. It was exactly this that she needed to talk about, the reason for her late-night phone call.

Ann also felt that the time was coming when Jenny may leave town—she could feel it even if Jenny couldn't.

* * * * *

THREE

Martin sat in his small flat above his office. It was an engineering business, in partnership with an old friend. Business had been good over these past years; it had made much for him, involving many types of contract work around the islands of New Guinea. However, things weren't going so well at the moment. He felt that his time there may be drawing to a close. He was restless, needed a change.

He had been back three weeks and had hardly stepped out of the office, relying on his team of boys to get the local work finished.

From his sitting room window, he could see *Sinabada* riding at anchor. Joe, his little mate, his boat boy was living aboard and keeping everything shipshape.

Martin reached across to the telephone and dialled a number; a recorded voice told him his call was being switched through, then the familiar burr of the phone ringing at the other end. The hour was late, she should be there—maybe out on a date or sound asleep? He glanced at the clock; it told him it was one in the morning. This was crazy, he started to return the phone to its cradle just as the burr stopped with a pip and he heard her voice.

'Hello!' Then tentatively another, 'Hello!'

'Jennifer, it's Martin Lord.'

Silence.

'Who?'

'It's Martin Lord from Jackson Bay Island, you know, north of Bougainville, New Guinea, we met in Cairns. I'm sorry, I did not mean to call so late, early eh! Whatever.'

Another silence.

'It's okay, Martin, I wasn't asleep. I didn't get in 'til late. How are you? It's lovely to hear from you. How did you get my number? Oh! Yes, forgot I gave it to you.'

Jenny stopped and took a breath and tried to collect her thoughts—get the butterflies in her stomach under control then!

'I'm so pleased you called; I was thinking of you.' Oh! She knew that was the wrong thing to say.

Another silence.

'Jenny, are you still there?'

'Yes, Martin.'

'Can I ring you another time?'

'Do you want to?' *A silly question, thought Jenny.*

'Of course, I'll ring you tomorrow at work, what's the number?

'439780.'

'Call you then, bye.'

The phone went dead, and Martin sat back and took a deep breath. Why had he done that at this time of the morning? He wanted so badly to make contact again ... was it a mistake? Martin reflected on the phone call for some time; had he actually made it, or did he dream it? Had this slip of a girl got to him, and would he really ring her tomorrow? He glanced at the number on his writing pad—489780. Well, we shall see.

Jennifer sat holding the phone, completely stunned; she suddenly dropped the handset back into place, turned the stereo on full blast, and went into the kitchen to make coffee. Her heart was singing, her thoughts in a turmoil, "*He had rung her, actually rung her!*" There was a chance, slim maybe, that Ann's suggestion to go north might be possible after all.

* * * * *

FOUR

Jenny bounced into work the next morning looking ten years younger and rearing to go. Geraldine, her receptionist, looked up.

'Hi! What happened to you? You look like the cat that just got the cream.'

'Oh, nothing,' Jenny replied, 'just feeling great. Had a good night's sleep for once,' which was a lie, she had hardly slept all night, but it didn't show.

Connie, her secretary, entered the reception area.

'Mr Harper called re finance figures on the D.P. development; John Austin from AMP—please call him; and Ann, reminding you of your luncheon engagement. I have set three appointments aside for later this afternoon, they are on your desk with some letters for your signature. Oh! The Big White Chief desires a meeting with you, so I have set that for 11 a.m.'

'Thanks Connie, you're a gem. Did Bob Cosgrove say what he wanted me for? Anyway, it doesn't matter,' she flung over her shoulder as she went into her office, not waiting for a reply, and not seeing the look that passed between her secretary and receptionist.

Suddenly it was 12:30 p.m. and Ann stuck her head in the office. 'Come on, Mummy!' (Ann loved to call Jenny *Mummy* at the office, denoting she was the mother hen and Ann one of her chicks) 'its lunch time, time to take a break.'

'Okay! With you in a tick, just had a session with the Big Man, so I need to finish off these notes while they're still fresh in my mind.'

'Meet you at the Lido in ten minutes.'

The Lido was a small restaurant just around the corner from the office. Ann had managed to secure a corner table out of the way of the main lunchtime crowd. She already had a couple of wine-and-sodas set up, and lunch ordered.

'Ordered a fish basket, nice and light, I know how you hate to eat,' Ann said as Jenny approached the table. 'Well, you look great today, not that you ever look bad. What's new?'

'Oh! Ann, been dying to talk to someone, I had a phone call last night—or rather this morning—it was after 1 a.m., I was dead to the world.'

'*He* called,' Ann finished for her. 'Yes, he did.' Ann lifted her glass in a silent toast, 'I hope you make it, Kid. God knows you deserve it.'

'Ann, I told Bob Cosgrove at our meeting this morning, that I may take a couple of weeks off at the end of the month. Can you talk to Jacquie Toms? I may take a trip.'

'Boy! Girl, you move fast; all this on the strength of one late-night phone call.'

Jenny opened her mouth to reply but the food arrived, so they ate in silence for a time, enjoying the food and the silent companionship. Jenny looked up and caught her friend watching her; she smiled raising an eyebrow in query.

'Jen, take it easy, don't push, he is after all a stranger to you and, from what little you have told me, quite a forceful character—don't get hurt.'

'Oh, come now, we were talking of a break, a short vacation. Even you said I needed it.'

'But you don't know anything about the place up there, or him, for that matter.'

'Then I will find out, won't I? Where is your sense of adventure?'

'Jacquie tells me her brother is always having trouble with the natives up there, they have been known to rape white women!'

'Now you are being dramatic, and it's quite a change from our conversation last night.'

'Well, I really hadn't thought much about it then, now I have, and it frightens me.'

'Look, Ann, quit worrying! I haven't gone yet, I am sitting across the table in the Lido Restaurant having lunch with my friend, for goodness sake. You have me up in the wilds somewhere already raped and murdered.'

Ann smiled at her friend, 'Okay,' she said, 'So I have a vivid imagination. I'll talk with Jacquie and see what can be arranged.'

'Ann, you look rather sad ... is something amiss?'

'Oh, nothing more than was before.'

Jenny knew Ann was having some troubles with her husband, and wondered if things were getting worse.

'Ann! You are always worrying about me, how are things with you and that husband of yours?'

'Nothing I can't handle, you have enough of your own problems to sort out.'

With that they dropped the subject and finished their meal in quiet friendship.

* * * * *

FIVE

Jennifer yawned, and stretched, a glance at the clock told her it was six o'clock, already another day gone by, three days since the call from Martin—how infuriating—not to mention frustrating!

Her disappointment that day had been agonising. Then she decided there was no way she would sit waiting for a phone call. Whatever had prompted the call in the first place had probably passed, *"So don't let it get to you, Kiddo!"* she said to herself.

Anyway, she had made up her mind; Ann had dutifully spoken with Jacquie and arrangements had been made for a two-week vacation on Jacquie's brother's plantation.

All she knew at this stage was that she was to book to Port Moresby, change planes for Lae, then a small inter-island plane would pick her up and take her to the plantation, where Don and Nicky lived.

The island was Nuala Plantation owned by Don and Nicky Toms and apparently there wasn't a lot to do: a small bay (good for swimming), some villages, and island-hopping to visit friends and/or other plantations.

The whole area was volcanic and was situated off the coast of New Britain; she had not dared to ask if it was anywhere near Jackson Bay and she had not found a map that showed either, but she did know where New Britain was. Nothing ventured, nothing gained; it would be an adventure anyway.

Having made the decision, she was feeling much better within herself, and even a little excited. Bob Cosgrove, on the other hand, had not liked it much, but conceded that he owed her a mountain of holidays, so had reluctantly agreed to hold the fort until she got back.

Now with a week to go before Jenny was due to leave, there were many things she had to attend to, apart from work. A glance at the clock told her a half hour had gone by, and with a half-hour drive ahead of her, she would not be home before seven o'clock.

With that she picked up her briefcase and took a last glance around the office to make sure all was okay, then she bolted for the door just as the phone rang. This time Jenny shrugged, *"Damn the phone, I'll not answer it this time,"* and headed for the lift.

* * *

The little twin-engine plane circled a cluster of islands below, and Jenny sighed, *"What a beautiful sight."* The land was so green and thick with tropical palms, the sea so blue with the occasional white beach and others looking so grey. Don explained that was because of the volcanic dust; however, he would explain more at a later time.

Her trip to Lae had been uneventful, apart from going through Customs at Port Moresby. It had taken an hour in the heat, and they had searched everything, carefully probing the satin bag that she kept all her panties in, plus all her photographs that she carried with her. Perhaps the natives did not see pretty underwear and they liked to look at pictures?

Then an hour's flight to Lae where Don Toms had been waiting to pick her up for the journey to the plantation. A nice guy, tall, rather on the thin side with a pleasant grin.

'You're Jennifer Lansing—I'm Don Toms, Jacquie's brother. Welcome to PNG! How do you manage to look so cool?'

'Air-conditioned aircraft, you should have seen me in Port Moresby,' Jenny replied.

'Oh! Moresby is a shocker of a place. If I go South, I try to go via Honiara and bypass the hassle of that place. Have you got much luggage?'

'No, only one small bag and my carry-all.'

'Great, like a woman who travels light.'

With a minimum of fuss, he had her aboard and before she knew it, they were off the ground and winging their way on a north-easterly course which would take them over the coast of New Britain.

Don explained he had bought the plantation some fifteen years back, and that Nicky was his second wife. Nicky loved the place, as he did, but found it a bit isolated at times; another white woman to talk to would be wonderful for her, she was really looking forward to it.

Jenny asked how they did their shopping and if they ever saw other white people.

Don further explained there were white people on the other islands close by, but that it could be weeks sometimes before they got together and, of course, there were yachts that called, stayed a few days, then left. The stores were either flown in or came with the copra barges.

'Look, Jenny!' Don's voice cut across Jenny's thoughts, 'The island to the left, that's Crater Island, Mola is to the east, the largest to the left again and with the two craters on the point, that's Jackson Bay Island.'

Jenny froze and tried to keep an even tempo to her voice, 'That looks like part of the mainland, it's so large.'

'Yes, but it is an island, takes about a half hour by boat to the mainland. We do most of our small shopping sprees at Jackson Bay, usually stay overnight when we go there. We will take you over there before you leave.'

With that, the little aircraft dropped its wing, banked to the left, straightened up and came into land on a small, grassed airstrip. There were rows of coconut palms lining either side of the runway, standing straight like a welcoming committee, as they taxied across to a grassed-roofed lean-to which, apparently, housed a petrol bowser and some other equipment. Two grinning natives came out of a large shed at the rear of the lean-to and ambled across, just as Don turned a switch and killed the motor.

Don yelled something fast and incoherent to the two boys, who replied in the same vein, then turned with a grin to Jenny noting her puzzled expression.

'That's Pidgin English; if you spend any time up here you will come to understand it.'

Jenny felt sure that she never would, but laughed anyway. In the next minute a jeep came boring down through the palms, along a track that Jenny had not noticed before. The jeep came to a grinding halt close to the plane, and a small, dark-haired woman literally flew into Don's arms.

Jenny stood by the plane, not the least embarrassed to witness such a tender greeting. When Don was finally able to extricate himself, he turned to Jenny, but before he was able to formally introduce her, Nicky threw her arms around Jenny and gave her a hug.

'Hi, you must be Jenny. I'm Nicky, welcome to Nuala. Don will bring your bags up to the house; come I'll show you around,' and she left dragging Jenny behind her. A glance over Jenny's shoulder saw Don with his hands on his hips and an indulgent smile on his face as if looking after a naughty, but well-loved, child.

By the time Jenny was seated in the jeep, heading for the plantation homestead, she was able to take stock of her surroundings and the woman seated alongside her.

Nicky was dark, vivacious, and about five foot one inches tall—much the same build and height as Jenny herself. The jeep was now climbing a gentle slope upwards between rows of coconut trees. They passed several small compounds with native women gathered around the huts, and Nicky waved breezily to them as they drove by.

'*Meris*—the native name for the women—belonging to the boys that work for Don,' Nicky explained.

Suddenly, they were at the top of the rise and the view was breathtaking, it was like they were sitting above the palm trees. The house was rambling, with a veranda almost all the way around it, and the heady perfume of hibiscus and frangipani hung in the air, making one feel soft and relaxed.

The main section of the home looked towards the open sea over the tops of the palms, which all appeared to be leaning across the water.

To the right could be seen other land masses— mainland or islands, Jenny didn't know. To the left was a small bay with, what appeared to be, two yachts anchored.

'Nicky, its beautiful!' exclaimed Jenny.

'I'm glad you like it, come on in, I'll show you the house and you can get settled; we can talk later.'

The entrance of the home opened on to a wide-open casual living area, tastefully furnished with soft rugs on parquetry flooring. Several casual sofa-like chairs were arranged conversation-style, and glowing timber framed the louvered windows, which were on two sides. Soft-white, sheer drapes framed the windows for maximum light, with the veranda roof creating the necessary shade and allowing the sea breeze to cool the interior. Ceiling fans gently circulated the cool air inside.

Two steps at the far end of the living area took you down into a country-style kitchen, where a central chopping table and an island bench for cooking allowed for maximum movement to all cupboards and outer benches. The draining-boards on either side of the double sinks were of scrubbed timber, as were most of the benchtops, thus giving the kitchen an old-world look.

Two native girls stood at the far end of the timber work-bench, apparently preparing some vegetables, and stopped what they were doing when Nicky and Jenny walked in.

'These are my two *haus-meris,*' explained Nicky. 'The shorter one is Nellie, and the taller one is Kelly. I call them that because I can never remember their native names.'

Nicky explained to the girls that Jenny was a houseguest and would stay for a couple of weeks, and both girls giggled profusely at Jenny, in reply. Jenny smiled back, then turned to follow Nicky who was rapidly moving back through the louvered door into the casual living room again.

'We will worry about the rest of the house later, let me show you to your room and the bathroom facilities, so you can relax.'

With that, Nicky bounded up four steps on the left side of the room, across what appeared to be a formal living area, down a corridor and flung open another louvered door. Jenny stepped into the room and was struck by the coolness, making her shiver.

'Oh, hell! They always insist on turning the air-conditioning on full blast,' Nicky said. 'I guess they think we are cold fish because our climate *back home* is supposed to be so much colder than this.'

Jenny laughed, and assured Nicky she really didn't mind, but after the heat outside it had been rather a shock to the system.

'Bathroom right through that door,' said Nicky pointing to another door leading off from the other side of the room, 'no one will disturb you; it services this room only.'

With that, she headed for the door they had just entered.

'I'll check on your bags, you make yourself at home, relax in a cool bath—you'll love it.'

Jenny stood alone in a rather lovely room, soft and sunny. She walked towards the glass French doors and opened them, the view from this side of the house was just as beautiful.

The air was cool under the veranda roof, and she took a few deep breaths of the light sea air and thought again of why she was here on this lovely island ... and of the blue eyes that haunted her.

A slight noise behind her made her turn and walk back inside in time to catch a glimpse of a native lad leaving the room. A quick glance around showed her he had just deposited her case at the foot of the bed. Well, she would investigate the bathroom and take Nicky's suggestion of a cool bath.

* * * * *

SIX

Cool, blue eyes looked down upon her, arms of steel wrapped around her, and a soft voice called her name, Jenny! Jenny! She moved slightly and turned, she was lying on a bed in a cool room which had grown dark, Nicky was standing by the bed.

'Hi, did you sleep well? Boy you must have been tired. Came by two hours ago and you were sleeping like a babe.'

'Oh! My Gosh! Nicky, what's the time?'

Jenny shook herself awake casting off the dregs of a dream. She had enjoyed the lovely cool bath, and had decided to lie down for a short while ... that was some hours ago, now it was dark outside, and the room was lit by the soft glow from the security lamp outside.

Nicky explained everyone has security lights outside to avoid being burgled; the soft hum she could hear was the generator down in the compound supplying them with electricity.

'Come on, Jen, hurry up,' called Nicky, 'Kai will be on the table shortly and I am dying to tell you what plans I have made for your stay.'

Jenny decided that *Kai* must be some sort of food, and made a mental note to ask about it as she swung her legs over the side of the bed and headed for the bathroom and her repair kit.

Kai, as Jenny learnt later, was indeed the word for food, but food in general, not any specific food.

* * *

A light breeze was blowing as the *Sinabada* rounded the point into the little bay just below Nuala Plantation. Martin had decided to make this his first call this time. Don had been on his back for quite a while to fix his main generator, so he figured it was time he made it a priority, besides he liked Nicky and Don Toms. Don and Martin had been friends for years, and Martin had been Best Man for Don when he married Nicky, so it was always good to stop in and chew over old times; a stay overnight would be most welcome, he thought.

'Masta!' called Joe, 'Masta Dons boat no stop.'

Martin looked up to see the little *Sea Nymph* was not at her mooring, but Don's speed boat was, so it would appear that Don was out on a pleasure sail, probably close by.

'Not to worry, Joe,' replied Martin, 'we'll go along Boi House, see what's cooking, have a look at the generator. Maybe Masta Don come back behind.'

He frowned, it was unusual for Don to be out midweek. They dropped anchor just off the small jetty. Martin loaded some gear into the dinghy while Joe got the outboard organised.

'Joe, I think there may be a storm brewing, tie up on the far side of the jetty. I'll go up to the house and see what's to do. You take the gear up to the compound. I'll be there shortly, just find out if Masta Don is home or not.'

As Martin walked up to the homestead, he could feel the wind freshen, he took another look at the darkening clouds above; yes, it looked like a storm was really coming up. He hoped Don and Nicky weren't too far afield to get caught in it.

As Martin approached the house, Kelly, one of the *haus-meris*, came running up to him, giggling and chattering. He had been tempted once a few months ago, thank God he hadn't—every native in the region would have known about it, not to mention the white folk. His name would have been nothing by the time the whites had got through with him; not to mention how bad for business it could have been.

He looked at Kelly, who was smiling up at him. She was fairly tall and slim for a native girl, looked like there was mixed blood in her away back. He wondered why he ever contemplated taking her to bed. Still, a man gets lonely and common-sense goes by the board.

He smiled at Kelly. 'Is Missus up at the house?' he asked.

'No Masta, Missus no stop. Missus go along boat with white lady visitor, maybe they come back tomorrow. Masta Martin stop along house tonight?'

'No Kelly, Masta Martin fix generator then go; I see Masta Missus belong you behind time.'

Kelly looked rather crestfallen but, nonetheless, turned and walked back to the house.

Well, Martin me lad! Let's get the generator fixed and leave before the storm hits, otherwise, I may be forced to stay the night, and that could be bad with both Don and Nicky away.

He looked up at the sky; yep, it could be a rough ride out, but he figured it could be rougher if he stayed.

* * * * *

SEVEN

The *Sea Nymph* had been sailing steadily, a nice easy sail, Jenny and Don standing at the helm. She was enjoying herself, it had been a glorious day so far, she and Nicky got along famously, and in the few days she had been with them they had become firm friends.

Jenny felt well, had scored a lovely tan—yes this was the life! She certainly would hate to leave, but now she sensed a change in Don's stance, a frown had formed on his brow, he called to Nicky.

'Honey, I think we will drop the sails and start the motor,' then turning to Jenny, 'how do you feel about taking the helm for a while?'

Jenny felt a tightening in her throat, her senses were right. To the east there looked to be a healthy storm bearing down on them.

'Of course, Don, just so that you remember it's a greenhorn you have on the helm.'

'You'll be right, Jen, just keep her bow pointed into the wind while Nicky and I get the sails down.'

Jenny swallowed the nervous lump in her throat and decided that, after all, it couldn't be any worse than steering a car. Don disappeared down the hatch and she heard the rumble of the motor come to life; the sails were flapping wildly now, and she caught a glimpse of Nicky trying desperately to pull in the small sail up at the bow. The next minute Don reappeared and started pulling the main. He yelled to Nicky something Jenny could not catch. She looked back and did not like what she saw; the sea was really starting to shake them around and the wind was getting pretty noisy, and the light was fading fast. Looking around, she saw Don and Nicky jumping into the cockpit beside her.

'We have a problem, girls,' Don said, 'the motor has shot a piston and we just snapped a forestay, which means we'll not get back tonight. We will have to use the storm jib; that should get us round that point up ahead and into that little bay round the back of the island, we should get enough shelter for the night. It won't be smooth, but it will be better than out here.'

Jenny asked, 'Isn't the storm jib a sail? Can't we sail back on just that?'

'No, Jen, the wind is wrong, and we have to go with the wind; as it is, it'll not be easy getting round the point.'

The rain was now starting to get pretty heavy, and for the next hour Jenny could think of nothing else but hanging on. Even the safety harness, that Don had insisted they all wear, did not make her feel any safer—she really felt quite helpless.

As suddenly as the wind came up so it died, and the little yacht seemed to just glide round the point into a tiny bay.

Nicky explained that they were really lucky as the bay was the back of their island, and in the morning they could row ashore and send one of the boys from the village to get a jeep. It would be a rough ride home. Jenny conceded that, at this point, she would much rather be roughing it in a jeep than being tossed like a cork on the open sea in a boat with a crippled motor. The rest of the night they rode at anchor, not too calmly, but certainly much easier than Don had expected.

Jenny awoke to the aroma of coffee brewing. Don looked across as she yawned and stretched.

'Sorry old girl, not a nice experience for your first sail.'

Jenny smiled, things always looked better in the light of day, and they were none the worse for the experience. She suddenly felt invigorated.

'Think nothing of it, I loved it. Like you say, it was an experience—perhaps one that I would not like to repeat too often.' She laughed, 'Boy, that coffee smells good,' and she suddenly felt very hungry.

'You girls get yourselves something to eat. I will take a hike back to the homestead, probably be gone about an hour or so.'

Jenny sat back and watched as Don paddled to the shore and thought how lucky Nicky and Don were to have each other, they were so suited—if that was the right expression.

'He's a great guy, isn't he?' Nicky's voice cut across Jen's thoughts.

'Actually, I figure you are both tops,' replied Jenny.

'You're not so bad yourself, Jen, can't think why some guy hasn't snapped you up.'

'Hey, I am hungry, let's eat.'

Nicky recognised the change of subject, agreed, and they both headed towards the galley.

* * * * *

EIGHT

The little speedboat bounced on the waves as it sped towards Jackson Bay Island. Sitting in the stern, Nicky was as happy as a sandboy at the prospect of doing some shopping. With only two more days of Jenny's stay, they decided to spend them on Jackson Bay so Jenny could shop for carvings and catch the jet to Moresby from there.

Jenny sat very quietly, contemplating the last two weeks; she really had enjoyed the change, and had not been bored once.

There would be loads to tell the girls, and some of it really was quite exciting, but with only two days to go she seemed destined not to cross paths with Martin Lord. She remembered her disappointment to find he had actually visited the Nuala Plantation while Don, Nicky, and herself had been battling the elements of the sea. Now as they approached his home island, she felt that she really would *not* like to meet with him this late in her holiday.

Fate could not be so cruel just as she was leaving again. Why did she not tell Nicky of her chance meeting with

Martin? She may have arranged another meeting, and at once she knew that was the reason for her not mentioning it, however silly. If they were to meet again then it had to be by chance or by *his* instigation.

* * *

Ann sat in Jennifer Lansing's office listening to Bob Cosgrove rambling on. It was the weekly staff meeting and she wished Jenny was sitting in the chair instead of Bob. Her thoughts wandered, thinking of Jenny and wondering if she was making out okay.

'I suppose it's too much to hope that Ann's mind would join us for this meeting, having managed to make it in body?'

Bob Cosgrove's sarcasm cut through Ann's thoughts.

'Sorry, Bob, got quite a bit on my mind just now. Jenny is due back in a couple of days, and there are a few unfinished deals she wants me to look into.'

'Okay, it's time we wound up this morning's proceedings anyway.' He looked rapidly around the staff, 'Any questions? Any problems?'

Everyone looked at him, it would make no difference if they had, he'd only say, 'Well, we'll leave that for Jennifer when she gets back.'

Ann knew the quality of her own work was falling; it had been a struggle for her to maintain her equilibrium because of her personal problems, and things seemed to be deteriorating since Jenny's absence. Ann knew also that if she didn't pull herself together soon her job would be on the line. She gathered up her notes to leave when a hand was gently laid on her shoulder.

Bob Cosgrove spoke kindly to her, 'Ann, I really don't want to interfere, but you look tired and troubled. Talk to Jenny about having a break just as soon as she gets back, will you?'

'Yes, Bob, I had planned to, things aren't going too well at home at the moment.'

Bob Cosgrove certainly had his moments, tough in business, and in many ways very hard, particularly if results weren't forthcoming; but he believed in the power of women in business, he believed in their ambitions. Not to give up, he always said; when women get down to it, they run rings round any man. For all that, he tried to understand the problems peculiar to them, at odd times being gentle and understanding, just like now.

Ann smiled at him, 'I'll be okay, Bob, thanks.'

Bob Cosgrove watched Ann Heywood leave the room, he had been sceptical when Jennifer had hired her, but in the end he agreed Jennifer's choice had been very wise. Ann was a good employee, extremely faithful to the company, and to Jennifer Lansing in particular. Jenny had an ability to bring out the best in people, the way she had shaped her office and staff was truly a credit to her, and it had been a big bonus for him over the years.

He knew a lot about the problems of these women who were tough in business, but were vulnerable and easily hurt in their personal lives. They needed particular types of men to back them.

He had seen Jennifer Lansing's marriage, and life, dissolve. For a while she had not handled it very well, but her fighting spirit came to the fore, and she fought back by transferring all her efforts to her work. So much so, he was concerned that she may burn out or have a nervous breakdown, or something of the kind. However, his worries appeared to be over in that area; now he could see another problem in Ann Heywood, and he doubted that she could show the same strength as Jennifer had. He heard a sigh, and brought his attention back to the problems at hand, neatly putting them all aside for Jennifer to handle on her return.

* * * * *

NINE

Don Toms was crossing the airport parking lot when a familiar voice called, 'Hi, Don! What's the hurry?'

He turned to see a tall, strong-looking man striding towards him. 'Great, Martin! How's things with you?'

The men shook hands vigorously, 'Come across to the lounge, I'll buy you a drink,' Martin said.

Neither men were great drinkers, both being workers, therefore standing apart from most of the island's whites.

'Sorry I missed you at Nuala, Martin, but thanks for fixing the problem generator.'

'That's okay, heard you had some problems with the *Sea Nymph* while entertaining a white lady.'

'Is that the rumour?'

Both laughed knowing full well how rumours spread round the small population they were a part of. Having reached the bar, and received their drinks, they settled at a small table on the end of the veranda. They had been great mates for many years, and enjoyed the few times they got together.

'Yes, the *Sea Nymph* ran into some problems, shot a piston in her motor, amongst other things, had to shelter in Back Bay for the night. I must say the women behaved splendidly.'

'Yes, I heard you had a houseguest friend of Nicky's, from South was it?'

'No, actually neither of us had met her before. A friend of a friend of my sister's down South, a big shot in finance, needed a rest—came up for a couple of weeks. Nicky loved her on sight, a really lovely person; we had a great time, name's Jennifer Lansing.'

'I say, Martin, are you okay?'

Don, who had been idly looking at his friend while talking, noticed Martin suddenly pale and almost choke on his drink.

Martin looked at his friend in disbelief, the sudden realisation dawned on him, the constant phone calls South to no avail, and all this time she had been close by, being entertained by two of his closest friends.

'Jesus Christ, man, do you know her? I've just put her on that plane not fifteen minutes ago.'

Martin started to tell Don his story, how he had met Jenny in Cairns, his constant battle with himself not to get involved with another woman, and then the phone calls over the last couple of weeks to no avail.

'You know she never said a word, though come to think of it, she always seemed very distant when your name came up. Oh! Shit, Martin, we are going to have to get you two together again, even if it's just to find out if there is anything there or not.'

'Hey! Steady mate, let's leave it. After all, she is on her way back South now, let sleeping dogs lie—for now anyway. Why didn't she mention knowing me? One can only assume she'd rather not.'

Don, of course, didn't subscribe to that way of thinking and decided the best way out was to tell Nicky *the story,* and the wiles of a woman would be able to solve that little problem.

Both men sat contemplating their own thoughts for a while before deciding they had best be on their way.

'Nicky will be disappointed at not seeing you, Martin. How about coming up to the plantation next weekend?'

'Okay, see you then.'

Don watched his friend walk slowly to his truck—he looked tired and a bit dejected. Yes, something had to be done, and Nicky was the one to arrange that. It wouldn't be easy, and may take some weeks, but we'll see.

Martin sat quietly behind the wheel of his work truck looking up at the sky as though willing the plane to return, then with a rueful smile on his face he started the engine and slowly drove out of the car park. The news that *Jennifer with the laughing eyes* had been actually staying with his close friends so stunned him it was difficult for him to get back into perspective, and the knowledge that she had made no attempt to contact him again puzzled him. Then, with a bemused smile he shrugged and decided *well, that was that.*

As the jet slowly taxied up the runway of Jackson Bay airstrip Jenny sat battling her emotions. Through the aircraft window she had watched the lanky figure of Don walking across the carpark to be greeted by another tall, slightly heavier set man. Her heart had missed a beat, she felt sure it was *him*, she had wished she could stand up and pull an emergency-stop cord so she could get off the plane.

After two weeks, to catch a glimpse of him *now* like that was unfair, and definitely fate was being very unkind. So, she struggled to convince herself that it wasn't him, and that she had had a great time, was feeling great, and would come back again—and next time fate would be kinder!

* * * * *

TEN

Three months had passed since Jenny had returned from her sojourn into the "wilds of New Guinea", to quote her work mates. Ann's home troubles had come to a boiling point, to the extent that she was now living in rented accommodation. A pleasant little home with lots of her treasures around her; she seemed to be coping pretty well, despite everyone's scepticism.

Ann had had a short holiday, but had found it harder to cope that way, and had begged Jenny to let her return to work. Jenny had finally agreed, and things seemed to be settling down fairly smoothly.

Jenny sighed as she drove down her driveway, she was back in the doldrums again. She would have to start cutting her working hours and begin accepting social engagements—anything to get back into the land of the living again.

Yes, she needed some excitement back in her life! Walking back up her driveway to check her mailbox— she let herself think again—she was surprised that she had not heard from Nicky and Don. On her return, Jenny had written a long letter thanking them for such a marvellous holiday, and to make her home theirs anytime they wished to have a break themselves. She hoped all was well with them. The phone was ringing as she grabbed her mail; at the front door she paused, why did she always race to the phone? Did she really expect a call from him after all this time?

Jenny opened the door and tossed the mail aside, as she reached the phone it stopped. She shrugged, and turned into the kitchen, probably one of her staff with a problem—anyway they would ring back if it was urgent. She put the kettle on to boil with cold water, nice and full, giving her time to shower while it was heating. The mail could wait, probably bills anyway.

Both the phone and the kettle were going nineteen-to-the-dozen when she stepped out of the shower; she grabbed the phone and asked the caller to wait, then made a mad dash into the kitchen to turn off the kettle, which was having a coronary on the stovetop. She was somewhat breathless when she got back to the phone.

'Hi, Mum! You sound like you have been running.'

It was her daughter, Danielle. Danielle had been married for some five years now, and had taken things pretty hard when her parents had broken up. There had been a slow coming around on Danny's part, but

Jenny now thought they had a great relationship growing.

'Oh! Danny, how are you? Yes, I had just got out of the shower and the kettle was going wild. What's your problem, darling?'

'Nothing, Mum, just wanted to say hello. I rang earlier, but you must have been still at work.'

'The phone was ringing when I came in, guess it must have been you.'

'Mum, I went to the doctors today, it would seem that you are going to be a grandmother soon.'

The silence was heavy, Jenny just stood there trying to comprehend what her daughter was saying.

'Mum! Aren't you pleased?' her daughter's voice cut across the shock waves in her brain.

'Eh! Yes, darling, of course, it wasn't the baby part that got to me, it was the *grandmother* part that threw me, it sounds sort of old.'

'Not you, Mother!' Danielle laughed, 'anyway must go; catch you for lunch on Friday.'

The phone went dead. Jenny hung up, she turned and looked at herself in the mirror. A grandmother—yet another milestone to cross. She really could not handle the mixed feelings, so decided to go tackle her mail and just not even think about it right now.

With a cup of coffee in her hand, she settled in a comfortable chair and proceeded to flip though her mail, there seemed to be a fair amount more than normal, but mostly circulars and rubbish mail. She spotted the stamp first, and a prickly feeling ran up her back, yes, it was from the islands. The neat, childish handwriting told her it was from Nicky, at last, and so strange to be thinking of them so strongly when she arrived home.

The letter began just like the person—breezy, and as though the mind ran faster than the hand—but what caught her eye was the reference to problems they were having, and Don's need for assistance with the office administration.

Jenny read the letter three times before it finally sank in, they were offering her a job for six months to a year, everything found and a reasonable income—not the salary she was currently on, but it would be enough.

Steady, Jenny! Just digest it first, think about it very seriously. This could be just what she needed to change her lifestyle—the chance, the break. If she did not burn her bridges back here at home, there would be plenty for her to come back to, if she needed to.

Jenny did not sleep well that night, her dreams were full of laughing, breezy girls and tall, serious men, pounding seas and sailing ships. She woke at four in the morning, feeling like she had just done battle with all the elements.

Jenny lay in bed looking out the window at the stars still to be seen at pre-dawn, and made her decision. She knew quite suddenly what she would do, and promptly fell into an easy, calm sleep.

* * * * *

ELEVEN

Bob Cosgrove's face was like stone as he stared at Jennifer from across his desk. Jenny was quiet, waiting for him to speak, reflecting on her decision to take six months off, and how telling her boss had, after all, come quite easy to her. Having made the decision, she had been most anxious to get it over with and had, in fact, dreaded this meeting with him.

Jenny glanced out of the window, it was a large office, high up, commanding magnificent views of this lovely city they lived in. She gasped and thought how calm she had been in telling him that she was prepared to leave all this ... for what? Very much the unknown.

The chair scraped back, and Bob stood up—he looked at her and said, 'Well, I guess I did burn you out, and I suppose there really isn't much I can do to dissuade you from your decision?'

Jenny slowly shook her head, but conceded that, mistaken or not, she was determined to go, and agreed to meet with him to discuss the finer details and the timeframe of her departure.

Closing the door to his office she turned to face her staff, they had to be told, and that was infinitely harder than telling Bob Cosgrove. There were other factors too, her family would be disappointed, Danielle would think she was running away from being a grandmother—the thought made her smile.

So, here she sat, not at all sure that the decision was the right one, but she knew something had to be decided, and yes, now was the time. She needed the break regardless.

The door of her office burst open, and Ann stood there wild-eyed.

'What's this I hear, YOU'RE LEAVING?'

Jenny motioned her to a chair, 'Sit down, and I will tell you all about it. Yes, it's true, just wish Bob had kept it quiet a little while longer, so that I could tell you all myself.'

Jenny quietly explained the offer of a job for six to twelve months to get Nicky and Don out of a tight corner, plus giving herself the change she really craved for.

Handing Ann Nicky's letter, 'Here, this will explain. I really need this, Ann.'

Ann looked at her friend and smiled.

'Yes, you do, and a whole lot more. Best of luck, Jen, hope you make it.'

* * *

That was three weeks ago, and all at work had been laid to rest and passed to a few to carry on while she was gone.

Things had been pretty hectic, but here she sat on the island-run plane heading for ... who knows what? Most of her work crew wished her well, Bob Cosgrove had mellowed towards her, but had still hoped 'til the end that she would change her mind. Now! She faced a new adventure, and still she saw in her mind's eye that stern, but gentle, face with the smiling eyes. Would she find peace and happiness at last? Would she even cross paths with him? Well, time would tell.

Jenny lay back and eyed the lovely scenery as the little plane winged its way towards Don's and Nicky's plantation. The lush green vegetation below painted a soft, comforting picture. Her Mum always used to tell her, "You must love green, its God's own colour," and looking at these tall, green mountains and soft valleys she could well believe it. Who else, but God, could make such a lovely scene?

Jenny awoke with a jolt—admiring the scenery was the last thing she remembered—the pleasant drone of the aircraft motor and looking at the peaceful scene below must have caused her to doze off. The jolt that disturbed her was the plane touching down on the plantation airstrip and taxiing to the disembarking hangar.

Well, here at last and she could see Nicky jumping up and down waiting for the plane to stop. Gosh, that girl had more vitality than most people she knew!

Jennifer started down the aircraft steps to the tarmac, waving to Nicky as she approached. Well, for what it's worth she was here, and all before her was a new beginning, and adventure of a kind.

* * * * *

TWELVE

"The end of a separation is to meet again"

— Old proverb

Nicky threw her arms round Jenny's neck.

'Boy! I am so glad you are here at last; we are going to have a great time together.'

Jenny laughed and said, 'I thought I was here to work, not be a companion.'

'Well, we will do that too. Okay, where is your luggage?'

'I gather being unloaded now! I'm the only passenger getting off here, the others are going on to other plantations.'

'Well, girl, let's get going!'

Jumping aboard the Land Rover, they took off for the homestead, about a ten minutes' drive down a dirt track in jungle-like territory. Jenny couldn't talk much; she was too busy hanging on for dear life! Nicky drove like a maniac, talking and laughing all the time.

Finally arriving at the homestead Jenny was exhausted, and ready for a catnap. Nicky had the native girls show Jenny to her room, the same one she had last time here. Very nice! The cool side of the house and, once again, the beautiful scenery of the landscape outside.

'Get yourself organised,' called Nicky, 'and we will have drinks on the veranda and fill you in on the work load we have for you.'

With that, Jenny hit the sack and fell into a deep sleep.

* * *

It had been three weeks since Jenny arrived on the plantation, and the whole time had been spent head-down slaving in the office with mountains of paperwork to complete. Now things were hopefully under control, and she could sit back and try to relax.

Maybe get some letters written for back home, let the girls know how things were progressing. It would be nice to explore this beautiful looking island.

Jenny sat up quickly, dropped her pen on the desk and decided that was enough for the day.

A bit hot for a walk, but maybe she had enough time to fly over to Rabaul to take a look around. She had been told it was a beautiful place. With that she went in search of Nicky.

* * *

Martin sat in his office wondering what he should do: go South and try to connect with Jenny, or write a letter inviting her to visit with him? Neither seemed to be a good idea. What to do? Work was slowing, as it usually did before the festive season. Well, maybe a trip to see Don and Nicky would pick him up from the doldrums. They were a fun couple, and always good to be around. With Christmas coming it would be nice to see them.

He wondered how things really were. None of the messages left on Jenny's phone had been answered, so things were looking pretty grim. Martin turned and picked up the phone calling Nuala Plantation. No answer ... well, time he took a look around at the various jobs at hand, to see that all was progressing okay. As he left the cool office, he again wondered what the hell he was doing trying to contact this lassie. He must realise by now that she wasn't going to answer him, and where in the hell were Don and Nicky? He had had no contact for such a time, well he would resolve that next time the plane came in, he may hitch a ride or even sail his trusty little vessel over to Nuala.

* * *

Jenny found Nicky flat out in the bakehouse.

'Hey! Nicky, can I get a ride over to Rabaul? I'd like to take a break and go see the place.'

'Hang on a minute,' Nicky replied, 'I think the plane may have left. If he hasn't, you can get a couple of hours over there before he has to head back. Sorry, I can't go with you, but Jeff Hanson, the pilot, will watch out for you, and it is an easy place to get around. Just stay away from the native villages. The people there are not very friendly if they think you are snooping. I will ring across to the airfield to make sure the plane is still there, and let Jeff know that you are on the way.'

Jenny waited in silence for the go-ahead; after a few minutes Nicky yelled.

'All okay, Jen, he will wait for you; I'll get one of the driver boys to take you over to the airfield.'

'Thanks, Nicky, see you when I get back.'

* * *

Jenny sat back enjoying the scenery. The flight was a pleasant one, with lots to see over water and land; it certainly was a beautiful country, she just hoped it would continue as such.

Jeff Hanson smiled at Jenny, and assured her he would not leave without her. 'So please try to stick to the schedule.'

Jenny smiled back. 'Thanks Jeff, I'll just take a walk around, have a look-see and come back—should be able to see heaps in two hours.'

The end of the runway was thick bush, *better not go there,* she thought. So she headed out away from the airport and what looked like a dusty road, walking between the shops or huts either side—boy was it hot! After some time she was very hot, and also thirsty, having drunk the little water she had with her.

She was thinking it would be a better idea to make her way back, when a bunch of *meris* came upon her. They all started jeering and taunting her, pushing her around.

Unfortunately she was not making much sense to them, and they just kept getting more and more aggro. Her blouse was ripped, and her scarf taken from her.

One of the women pushed her so hard she fell to the ground. It was then she started screaming at them to leave her be, but the more she fought them the worse it got.

Finally, she broke loose from them and started running like a mad thing. Which way to the airport? She really hadn't taken much notice as to which way, she was so frightened she had run blindly away from them. What had she done to upset them so?

* * * * *

THIRTEEN

Jenny didn't know how long she had sat there in the blazing sun, not her usual, calm self. Why had she been so frightened? Did they really mean to harm her? Well, sitting here wasn't helping, she had to find her way back to the airport, otherwise she would not make it back to the plantation.

Jenny stood up, stumbling a bit, and turned to take stock of her surroundings. Nothing was familiar, so she started walking towards one of the volcanoes, she knew they tended to overlook the runway.

Sometime later—unsure how long she had been walking—she heard a car coming from behind her. What now, was she walking in the wrong direction? The car, or rather a ute of some description, stopped alongside her.

'Hey Missus, you walk in this heat, you will get sick.'

Jenny turned to see a young man, with a very cheeky grin, leaning out of the window of the vehicle!

'Can I help in anyway? Perhaps give you a lift to wherever you want to go?'

Jenny looked up and saw a pair of kindly eyes looking at her with concern, but with merriment on his face.

'My, you look like you have been through a war zone. Are you okay?'

'Yes, I could really do with some help, I was walking around looking at the terrain, and these natives jumped me. I could not understand what they were yelling at me, unfortunately I started fighting back ... guess I came off worse.'

'No worries, lady, I'll get you back. Where would you like to go?'

'Please, can you drop me at the airport? I think the pilot is waiting to fly me back to the plantation.'

'Are you off a plantation?'

'No, not really, just doing a bit of work for the Toms' on Nuala. Sorting out some accounting, and taking a break from down South.'

Jennifer turned and looked at this young man asking all the questions, 'And what do you do?' she asked.

'I work for an electrical engineering company, just around the back bend. On my way to the airport to pick up some parcel delivery.'

'Great!' Jenny said, 'just where I want to go, need to catch the plane. Hope he is still waiting for me ... that's if you don't mind dropping me off?'

'Not at all, buckle up!'

Jenny lay her head back on the head rest and started to think about a beautiful man called Martin, she turned her head and looked at the young man driving.

'You didn't tell me your name? I guess you do have one?'

'Oh! Yes, its Ian, and can I ask what your name is?'

'Yes, I am Jennifer, but most people call me Jenny—at least all my friends do.'

'So, can I call you Jenny?'

'Yep, go for it!'

At that point, the truck rounded a bend in the road and the airport was just ahead of them. Ian parked alongside a lean-to serving as a terminal for ticketing, etc.

Jenny jumped out and said, 'Many thanks for the lift!' and made a dash for the terminal.

Ian watched her go and thought how he would have liked to see more of her.

'Have a good flight!' he yelled. Jen looked back, waved and smiled, almost tripping over someone's case sitting on the ground.

'Whoops, so sorry,' she said and headed across to the plantation plane, which appeared to be standing in the same spot as she left it earlier.

'Gosh! Jenny, what happened to you?' This was from Jeff, the pilot.

'Well, I guess I ran into a bit of trouble with a bunch of native women. I don't understand the reason, but I ended up running from them. A young man gave me a lift, his name was Ian.'

'Oh! Yes, Martin Lord's offsider—nice guy,'

Jenny stood there stunned.

'Hey, Jen, are you okay? You look like you have seen something out of a horror movie!'

'No, Jeff. I was hoping to catch up with Martin Lord, but didn't know the connection ... can you give me minute?'

'Yes, sure.' Jenny took off back to Ian, who was still waiting by the truck.

'Hey Ian, just heard you work with Martin Lord. I met him once; can you give him a message from me?'

'Okay!'

'Tell him you met me, and I said 'hello', and I would like to catch up before I head back south.'

'Will do, Jen. I will get him to ring you at the plantation.'

'Great, thanks.'

Jenny ran back to the aircraft feeling a mite happier, and hoping this would end the "ifs-and-buts-and-maybes".

* * * * *

FOURTEEN

On returning to the plantation, Jenny was in a very happy mood, and hoping everything good was going to happen. Then, she was greeted with Nicky's glum face.

'Hey! Friend, what's the problem? Have I been away too long with heaps to be done?'

'Oh! No, Jenny, but I have some pretty bad news for you from South, suggest you take a seat and listen to me.'

'Wow, that sounds pretty ominous.' Jenny looked at her friend, whom she thought had some nasty problems to get sorted with Jenny's help.

'Jenny, it concerns your friend, Ann, down South.'

Jenny sat looking at Nicky, suddenly realising the bad news was for her, not Nicky.

'What happened? Nicky, tell me.'

'Well, it would seem Ann's husband bashed her up, and Ann is in hospital, not expected to pull through at this stage—she is asking for you.'

'Oh, my God! I have to go to her. Can you spare me for a while, a few days—maybe a few weeks?'

'Yes, Jen, of course we will manage, but please come back to us if you can, soon.'

Jenny sat dumbfounded, not really knowing what to do. Nicky said, 'Take care friend, we will do all we can to help. I called and booked you on a plane South, a.m. on the morrow, so take your time and get a few things together. We will do the rest.'

Jenny looked at her with gratitude; for the first time in ages she was at a loss, she really must pull herself together, this really was no time to lose it.

Jenny slowly got up and left the room. Nicky's eyes followed her with some sadness, she hoped that Ann would pull through and all would be well when Jenny saw her.

Jenny made her way to her room, the lovely room that had been her haven for all these weeks. She looked around trying to get herself together ... she must try to get some sleep so she could be as bright as possible to see Ann.

The next day was a hurried one, getting all things together, leaving her office and bedroom as tidy as possible, then leaving her lovely retreat and heading for the airport. How she hated leaving the Toms, but Ann needed her, and this was what she had to do.

The flight south was uneventful. As usual there was chaos at the arrival terminal, however, Bob Cosgrove was there to meet her and had nothing new to report, except that things were not good, there had been no improvement.

'I'll go straight to the hospital if you don't mind, Bob, I need to speak with her and let her know I am here.'

'Yes, she would like that, I'll drive you and wait to take you home.'

'Oh! Thanks, Bob, I'll try not to keep you waiting too long.'

With that, Jenny sat back in silence on the short drive to the hospital. When she arrived at the hospital, she had a strange premonition.

'What floor is she on Bob?'

'Three, I believe, Jenny. But we can ask at the reception.'

So, heading for the reception Jenny was waylaid by a nurse she knew.

'Oh! Hi Christine, do you have news of Ann?'

'Hi, Jenny, I have to say it's not good to see you at this time. Can you please come this way? I would like to talk with you before you go up.'

'Is all, okay? Is she going to make it?'

'No. I am *very* sorry, but your friend passed away about twenty minutes ago, and the doctor is with her now.'

Jenny stood there stunned, how could this be, *"Oh! Ann, could you not wait just a few more minutes?"* Jenny's thoughts where in a turmoil. She looked at Christine, and said in a very small voice, 'May I see her please?'

'Yes, but can you wait a few minutes while I check with the doctor? I am sure it will be alright.'

Jenny stood silent, lost in a forest of gloom, she had never had such feelings before. She thought about all the good times, then things started to come back into focus, and she started to think more clearly.

Just then the nurse came back, 'Miss Lansing—Jenny— the doctor says you may go in, but just for a few moments. Ann's family are on their way to make arrangements, and there will be a few people milling around. We have to try to keep things to a minimum.'

'Thanks, Christine, I won't be long,' Jenny turned to Bob Cosgrove, he nodded and gestured for her to move on in. He would be okay and would wait for her.

Jenny moved silently into the room where Ann lay looking so still, small, and very pale under the bandages around her head. Poor dear, she must have been in pain.

Jenny moved towards the bed and took one of Ann's hands. My God! She was so cold; she touched the side of her face and bent and kissed the part of her cheek where there was no dressing.

'Ann, Godspeed my love, be happy where your spirit goes, I am sure we will meet again in another life.' With that said, and as the tears were falling on the sheets, she stood up, released Ann's lifeless hand, and with one more look, turned and left the room.

* * * * *

FIFTEEN

Jenny, put the key in her front door and let herself into the peace and quiet of her lovely home, but how lonely she felt. Moving to the kitchen, she needed to have a coffee and maybe a good cry to relieve the pressure of the sadness. Bob had been very good and helpful, but she now knew she wanted to go back to New Guinea and to the lush green there, to the friendly people and ... maybe into the arms of an aloof stranger. Just then the phone rang.

'Aunt Jenny,' said a tearful Amanda. Amanda always called her aunt, she had known her ever since she was born, and Ann had insisted *aunt* was who she would be.

'Yes! Amanda, how are you managing?'

'I think okay now, it is taking a lot of getting used to. I really just wanted to know how you are, you and Mum were always so close.'

'I know, darling, how are the arrangements?'

'We are holding the service and cremation the day after tomorrow. It's quick, I know, but they are being really good about it, and we don't want to keep everyone waiting—they have homes to go back to—so this will save them coming back in a couple of weeks' time.'

'Good idea, call me when you have all the details to hand. Cheers, darling, and be brave, love you.'

With a deep sigh, she sat and contemplated her immediate future. There was much to do again before she could leave, she would miss Ann so much—after all, she was the closest and oldest friend she had. However, the arrangements had been brought forward, which was good, just over a week since it had happened, so that was great management on everyone's part.

Ann's family had said they would keep her informed as to the funeral and internment, and so they had. God, how was she going to get through these next few days? She must ring Nicky and let her know when to expect her back.

* * *

Martin sat by his phone unable to comprehend that, once again, their paths had veered off in different directions. Is this his fate?! The illusive destiny that keeps teasing him!

Martin had been absolutely amazed that Ian, his offsider, had in fact given Jenny a lift to the airport and brought back a message from her. Now he finds out she has left to go South under tragic circumstances! Well, he would find out the details and try to go down and support her, in some measure.

Should she turn him away then he will know all is finished, so to speak. Martin got up to leave the office when the desk phone rang.

'Hello! Martin Lord here!'

'Oh! Martin, Don Toms. Nicky just told me the news, and Jenny has gone South. I believe she didn't make it in time, Ann passed away just before she got there, but the funeral arrangements have been made, it will be held next week.'

'Yes, Don, thanks for letting me know, I am going to go down and see if I can be of any assistance to Jenny—that's if she will see me.'

'That's great, man! I'm sure she will appreciate it. Keep me posted just in case I can assist in any way.'

'Sure will, mate. Thanks for the call.'

* * * * *

SIXTEEN

Where you go — I will follow.

Jenny sat in the church and followed the service; it was a nice ceremony—very fitting for the lovely person Ann was.

Now the congregation moved forward to pay their respects, and to place flowers and the ilk on the coffin; this was a poignant moment in the service. Giving their respects brought home to all of them just what had happened, and the dear friend and relative they would miss so much.

The coffin was then carried out to the awaiting hearse where it would be taken to the private cremation.

Jenny rose and walked slowly outside, so many people spoke to her, but she could not comprehend anything. She was walking in a daze, not really aware of her surroundings, so she kept a small smile on her face and just nodded, hoping they would all understand.

Quite suddenly she had an overwhelming feeling that something wonderful was about to happen. Someone took her hand and held it, her whole being relaxed as she looked around to see those lovely, blue, kind eyes looking at her with great concern ... and then she heard *the voice*.

'Hi, Jen! Are you okay, and is it alright for me to be here?'

Out of all this sadness and misery *he* had come to her! She smiled and lay her head against his shoulder, there were no words to say that could fully explain her feelings of love for him. He had come to her in her time of need, and that was explanation enough for both of them.

La Fin

* * * * *

EPILOGUE

It was six months since Ann's funeral and the meeting of two loves.

Jennifer Lansing stood on the bow of the yacht, *Sinabada,* and enjoyed the smooth, gentle rock of the little sailing boat. Oh, how things had worked out for them both and, thank God, for the tenacity of this strong, gentle man to not give up.

They had been married in Cairns just three weeks ago, and this was the promised honeymoon: just to sail "all over" for a week or two before settling down to a blissful marriage. Was that too naïve to hope for?

Well, did it matter? Destiny had been good to them so far, and there looked to be a good future ahead. Marriage is like sailing, it will have its ups and downs, like a gentle rocking in the lull of a quiet bay, and also the rough of a stormy sea.

Jenny looked back towards the stern and smiled; she would enjoy every minute of it!

Martin looked up and caught Jenny's glance, and smiled too. It had been a long and arduous journey for them both, but they had survived, and in doing so had found each other, and their destiny. He had asked Don, and Don had agreed to be his Best Man, it had been a lovely service, nice and simple, and Jenny would continue to assist Don and Nicky where possible, while they were in PNG.

Oh! How lucky was he, to have earned a wife such as she! Did *Luck* really have that much to do with it, or was it just plain *Destiny*? What more would you want out of life than to learn the lessons taught and end up on the right side.

* * * * *

A VIKING'S TALE

By The Scurvy Dogs!

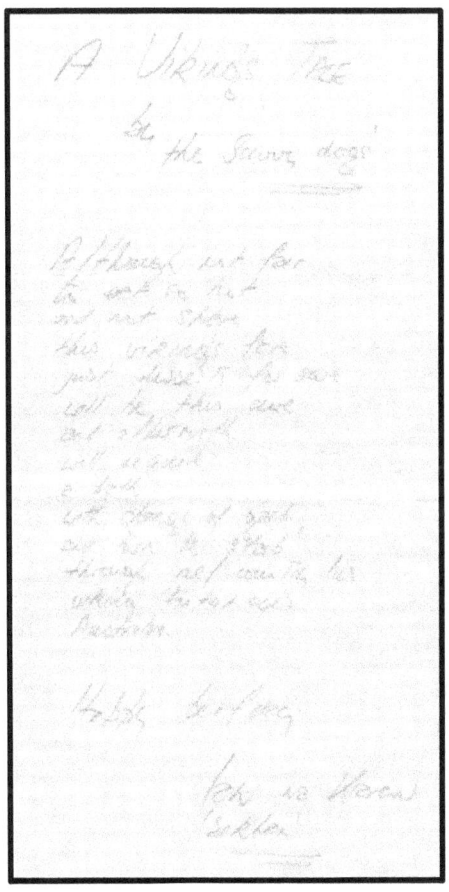

Although not fair
to eat so hot
and not share
this viking's fare
just desserts for sure
will be this cure
and aftermath
will require a bath
with change of garb
and turn to starb'
through reef country
lies
viking tinted eyes
— Australia.

Happy berfday
Ian and Karen
SV Sekhan

ABOUT THE AUTHOR

Judith (Judi) Waller was born in Charing Cross, London, England in 1935, and lived in Feltham, Middlesex until the start of World War Two in 1939.

Judi, and her sister Ann, were sent to a convent run by Nuns for some of the war term. Prior to the breakout of the war, the convent was an orphanage, but at the onset of war with Germany the doors were opened to all children—including those who were left behind due to their parents' obligations to the war effort—to provide a safe haven in the country away from the devastation of the cities.

After the war, Judi, with her family, moved to Falmouth in Cornwall, South England. In 1949 she emigrated to Australia with her parents, sister, and brother.

Judi's professional career spanned across Australia and Papua New Guinea. She attained a real estate license and ultimately owned and ran her own real estate agency in Canberra, Australian Capital Territory.

Judi also attained a Company Directors certificate through the University of New England in Armidale, New South Wales. At that time, Judi was one of the few females to complete a Company Directors course.

One of the many things Judi aspired to was to become a published author. Finally, having retired, she fulfilled that dream with the publication of her first book, *The Tales End* in 2021.

Having had one book published, it gave Judi the courage to complete a novella that she started writing some twenty years earlier, culminating with the publishing of *The Perfect Stranger*.

More from Judi Waller . . .

The Tales End — an anthology of short stories.

Available at judi.waller@bigpond.com

eBook available from Amazon www.amazon.com